ISBN# 9780692694824

Email the Author: Angelo@FreddytheFerry.com

Visit www.FreddytheFerry.com for special updates and merchandise.

Other Books by Author Available on Amazon.com:

The Big Bad Blow Fish

To My 3 children Angelo, Alyssa, and Aria:

Thanks for always asking me to tell you a story.

Freddy the Ferry

Thousands of people ride the Staten Island Ferry each day,

Each of them going different ways, some to work, and some to play.

From far and wide the visitors appear,

Waiting for a ride to the nearest pier.

The harbor holds a statue that stands with grace,

And Ellis Island holds the names of people from all over the place.

There is not just one Ferry, that would not be enough,

And all of the Ferries are confident and tough.

But the newest is named Freddy, you see,

He's a bit smaller and full of curiosity.

Because he is new, Freddy stays at the terminal the most,

But he wanted to float and be a great host!

Freddy paced back and forth, bubbling the water far and near,

When he looked at his friend Tony and said, "I wish I could get out of here!"

Now Tony was not a ferry, but a tugboat so buff,

He was strong, and smart, and fearless, and rough!

"You just have to be patient," Tony said with a smile.

"But I'm ready to work! I've been waiting a while!"

Freddy wanted to be the best boat on the water,

He'd be faster and smoother than the fastest sea otter.

The people would rave, "He's the best ferry here!"

Freddy said, "I know I can do it! I have nothing to fear!"

Just about then another tugboat pulled in to dock,

Tommy was pushing another ferry with a bump and a knock!

"What's wrong with you Frankie?" Freddy asked, scared.

"I've got some old rust spots that I need repaired."

Frankie winked at Freddy and said, "You'll need to get ready,

Remember to keep yourself nice and steady."

All of the sudden, something happened inside,

Freddy was nervous about giving his very first ride.

"What if I'm too slow, or maybe too fast?"

"What if I drop off my first passenger last?

What will I do if I get lost at sea?

Or worst of all: what if I end up in New Jersey!"

Frankie the Ferry knew what to say,

He had to give Freddy some confidence, today!

"There are four thousand people waiting over there,"

"Some fuzzy, some bald, some with crazy hair,

But each of them has a certain place to go,

And you are the only one who will know:"

"How to get them from the St. George Terminal here,

All the way over to the Manhattan Terminal pier."

Tony turned to Freddy and looked him in the eye,

"Don't worry my friend, I will be nearby."

"I'll do it!" said Freddy, his head high in the air.

I will take all of them all the way there!

Five miles is nothing for a strong boat like me,

And I will show the tourists what they want to see!"

One by one the passengers boarded the boat,

And Freddy was strong and kept afloat.

Once they were all ready and little time had been spent,

Freddy tooted his horn and off to Manhattan they went.

Freddy was still a little nervous inside,

But all of the passengers were enjoying the ride.

Past the Statue of Liberty the strong ferry flew,

When the Liberty Ferry stopped and said, "Hey! You're new!

"My name is Lisa! Welcome to the fleet!

Be careful! You wouldn't want to crash into Lady Liberty's feet!"

She took her passengers to visit the Statue so tall,

So far Lisa was the nicest Ferry of all!

Freddy was almost to the terminal when he got a surprise,
Another boat zoomed right past his eyes!

It was Tina the Taxi, and she was very fast,
There was no way that she'd ever be last.

He saw the terminal, and his big ferry boat hopped,

As he floated brave and strong until he pulled in and stopped.

The passengers rushed off to start their day,
All of them with something different to say.

Staten Island Fer

"That was a nice ferry," one woman grinned.

"Yes, it was the smoothest one I've been in."

Another man smiled and said, "This ferry was quick!"

As a little boy waved goodbye and gave his lollipop a lick.

"You did it!" said Tony, "It was perfect, I'd say.

Now you have to do it one hundred more times today!

"One hundred more times!" Freddy was scared a bit.

But then more passengers climbed on and started to sit.

"I'm ready!" said Freddy as he pulled back across the bay.

"I've got plenty of energy to do this all day!"

And that was how Freddy got his start as a ferry,

But there were some days not so happy and merry.

Freddy has lots of adventures, you see.

Too many to tell in just one little story!

Another adventure is waiting; so, just open the book.
You will find Freddy! Hurry, go take a look!

Made in the USA
Middletown, DE
15 September 2016